READ YOUR

Disney
PLANES
FIRE & RESCUE

eBOOK TODAY!

Fly high with Dusty Crophopper as he explores a new career full of daring and adventure. Visit www.planesbundle.com.

© Disney

Easy-to-follow instructions inside!

Open Here

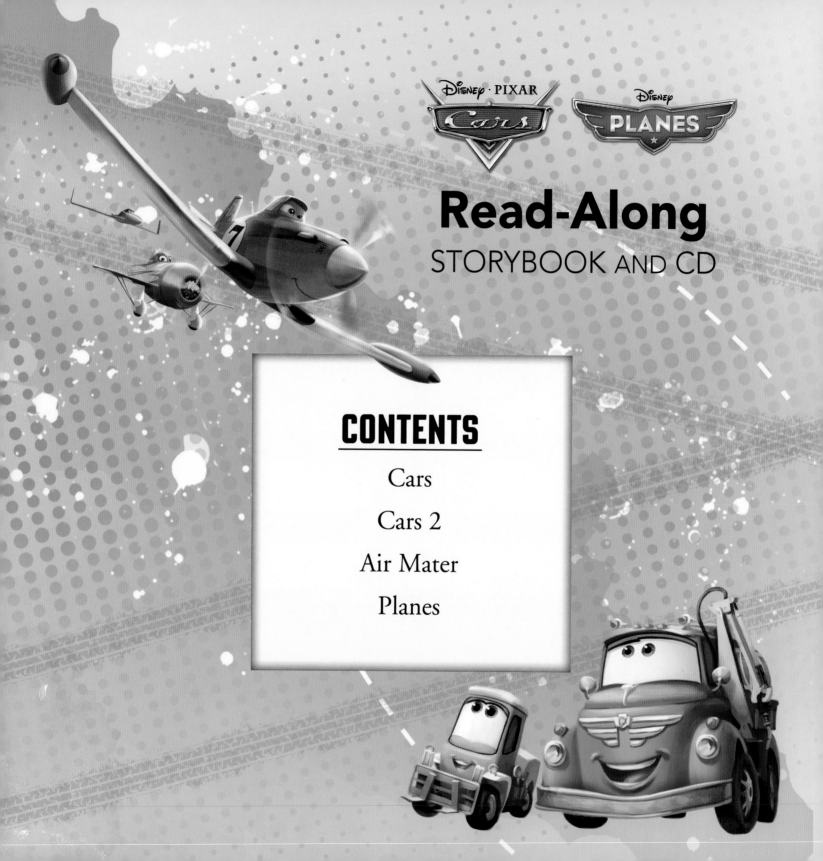

Read-Along
STORYBOOK AND CD

CONTENTS

Cars

Cars 2

Air Mater

Planes

Read-Along
STORYBOOK AND CD

Lightning McQueen is fast. But sometimes it takes more than just speed to win a race. To find out if Lightning has what it takes to become a real champion, buckle your seat belts and read along with me from your book. You'll know it's time to turn the page when you hear this sound. . . .

Start your engines. It's go time!

Read-Along Storybook Produced by Randy Thornton and Ted Kryczko; Co-produced and Engineered by Jeff Sheridan; Adapted by David Watts
Illustrated by the Disney Storybook Artists, ℗ 2009 Walt Disney Records/Pixar © Disney/Pixar. All rights reserved.

It was the final race of the season, and Lightning McQueen was in the lead. But on the final turn, his rear tires blew out. It was a three-way tie!

A tiebreaker race was to be held in California in one week. So Lightning drove into his trailer and set off with his driver, Mack.

"California, here we come!"

Later, after hours of driving, a weary Mack started to doze off. Some pranksters began nudging him back and forth.

In the jostling, the trailer door opened. A sleeping Lightning slipped down the ramp of the trailer! Jolted awake, Lightning looked everywhere for his driver.

"Mack! Mack! Mack, wait for me!" He followed a truck off the Interstate, but then he realized it wasn't Mack.

Confused and lost, Lightning wound up racing through the small town of Radiator Springs, where he lost control and crashed into just about everything. When it was all over, Lightning wound up caught in telephone wires. The road was ruined.

A police car named Sheriff glared at him. "Boy, you're in a heap of trouble."

The next morning, Lightning found himself in traffic court.
The doors burst open, and the judge, Doc Hudson, rolled in.
"All right, I wanna know who's responsible for wrecking my
town, Sheriff." But Doc took one look at Lightning and stopped
short. "Throw him outta here, Sheriff. Case dismissed!"

Just then, a Porsche entered. "Sorry I'm late, Your Honor."
It was Sally, the town attorney. "Come on, make this guy
fix the road. The town needs this."
Reluctantly, Doc changed his mind and Lightning was
sentenced to remain in Radiator Springs and fix the road.

Later that day, Doc introduced Lightning to Bessie, a road-paving machine. "So we're gonna hitch you up to sweet Bessie, and you're gonna pull her nice."

As soon as he could, Lightning zoomed away. "Woo-hoo! Good-bye, Radiator Springs!" But he didn't get far before he ran out of gas. Lightning realized that the sooner he fixed the road, the sooner he'd make it to California. Within an hour he had finished the job—but he hadn't done it well.

Doc pulled up. "The deal was you fix the road, not make it worse. Now scrape it off."

"Hey, look, Grandpa, I'm not a bulldozer. I'm a race car."

"Whoa! Then why don't we just have a little race. Me and you. If you win, you go and I fix the road. If I win, you do the road my way."

Later, at a dirt track outside of town, the two cars sat at the starting line.

Lightning took off like a bullet, while Doc slowly started down the track. But Lightning sped into a turn, lost control, and drove into a cactus patch.

Doc easily won the race. "You drive like you fix roads—lousy."

After losing to Doc, Lighting worked through the night on the road. By morning, there was a beautifully paved new section of road. Lighting headed off to the dirt track.

He wanted to try the turn he'd missed the day before. He tried again and again, but he kept skidding out. Then Lightning saw Doc watching. "If you're going hard enough left, you'll find yourself turning right."

Lightning scoffed. What did Doc know about racing?

The next morning, Lightning was back at work on the road. All of the townsfolk were so inspired by how wonderful it looked that they began cleaning up their shops. The whole town was starting to look brand-new, but Lightning was still dirty. Sally got him all cleaned up.

That night, Mater the tow truck snuck Lightning out of town for some fun. Mater showed Lightning his crazy backwards-driving moves.

"Whoa! That was incredible! How'd you do that?"

"I'll teach you if you want."

"Maybe I'll use it in my big race."

The next day, Lightning wandered into Doc's garage.
Just then, Doc entered. "Sign says STAY OUT."
"You have three Piston Cups. You're the Hudson Hornet!"
Lightning realized that Doc had been a famous race car.
But Doc didn't want to talk about it and slammed the door
in Lightning's face.

Later, Sally invited Lightning to go for a drive. The view was breathtaking. But on the nearby Interstate, cars just sped on by. Sally told Lightning all about the town in its heyday, and of her dream of returning Radiator Springs to its former glory.

A little while later, Lightning came upon Doc roaring around the dirt track and was truly impressed.

"You've still got it! Under the hood, you and I are the same."

"We are not the same, understand?" Doc told Lightning how the racing world had left him long ago, after he had a big crash.

"Doc, I'm not them."

"Oh, yeah? When was the last time you cared about something except yourself, hot rod? Just finish that road and get outta here!"

Early the next morning, the townsfolk awoke to find the road finished and no sign of Lightning.

Then Lightning appeared. He said he couldn't leave without getting new tires from Luigi and Guido. They were thrilled!

"Our first real customer in years!"

Lightning bought something from every shop in town.

Lightning even had a surprise for Sally. On his cue, the townsfolk turned on their newly repaired neon signs. Sally was amazed. The town looked like it did in its heyday.

Suddenly, vehicles swarmed into town. In an instant, Lightning was surrounded by reporters. "Will you still race for the Piston Cup?" Mack pulled up and urged Lightning to come with him. Lightning tried to say good-bye to Sally, but no words would come.

She spoke for him. "Thank you. Thanks for everything."

After Lightning had gone, Sally learned that Doc had called the reporters to tell them where Lightning was. He knew that would get Lightning out of town. "It's best for everyone, Sally."

A few days later, as Lightning raced in the big race, all he
could think of was Sally. By the time he snapped out of it, he was
heading straight for the wall! He hit his brakes hard and spun
into the infield. He felt like giving up.

Then he heard a familiar voice. "I didn't come all this way to see you quit." It was Doc. He was in pit row with a bunch of the Radiator Springs gang! Doc had realized he'd been wrong about Lightning. Now Doc wanted to help him win.

"Kid, get back out there."

Back in the race, Lightning was more than a lap behind. But he caught up by using some fancy driving.

Then, on the final lap, Chick Hicks bumped him and sent him spinning. But Lightning used Doc's "turn right to go left" move and shot into the lead!

Then, as Lightning raced for the checkered flag, he heard the crowd gasp. Chick had rammed into The King, a legendary race car about to retire.

Lightning saw The King in the infield. It reminded him of Doc's big crash. Instead of crossing the finish line, Lightning hit the brakes and went back to help.

The King was confused. "What are you doing, kid?"
"I think The King should finish his last race." Lightning pushed
The King across the finish line. Lightning had finished in last
place, but he had shown everyone what makes a real champion.

A few days later, Lightning headed back to Radiator Springs. He told Sally about his plans to set up his racing headquarters there.

"Really? Oh, well, there goes the town." And with that, Sally raced off.

Lightning happily took off after her. "Yeah! *Ka-chow!*"

Read-Along
STORYBOOK AND CD

Mater joins his best bud, Lightning McQueen, for a race through Tokyo, Italy, and London. To find out what happens when Mater is mistaken for a secret agent, read along with me in your book. You will know it's time to turn the page when you hear this sound. . . .

Let's begin now. Start your engines. It's go time!

Read-Along Storybook Produced by Ted Kryczko and Jeff Sheridan; Assistant Engineer: Frank Turbé; Adapted by Chase Wheeler
Illustrated by the Disney Storybook Artists. ℗ 2011 Walt Disney Records/Pixar © Disney/Pixar. All rights reserved.

Finn McMissile and Holley Shiftwell stood on the second floor of the Tokyo Museum. They stared down at the party below. It was the night before the World Grand Prix, and the fastest cars in the world were all there.

But Finn and Holley weren't watching the racers. They were British secret agents, and they were looking for an American agent who had some important information.

Down at the party, Mater the tow truck and his best friend, the famous race car Lightning McQueen, were talking with Miles Axlerod, who was in charge of the race. Mater had been excited all night, and it kept getting him in trouble.

When Lightning spotted some oil by Mater, he got upset. "Mater, you have to get ahold of yourself! You're making a scene."

Mater was embarrassed. "But I never leak oil. Never." He hurried off to the bathroom.

As he left the bathroom stall, Mater interrupted a fight. One of the cars in the fight was the American agent.

When Mater wasn't paying attention, the secret agent saw his chance. He planted the top secret information on the tow truck.

A second later, the two other cars chased Mater away. "Get outta here!"

Out in the hallway, Holley stopped Mater. She spoke to him
in a quiet voice. "When can I see you again?"

Mater was surprised. "Well, let's see. Tomorrow I'll be out
there at the races." He thought Holley wanted to go on a date.

But Holley didn't want a date. She knew Mater was carrying
secret information. She thought *he* was the American agent!

The next day was the first race of the World Grand Prix. Lightning McQueen zoomed around the track as Mater and the rest of the crew cheered him on from the pit.

Suddenly, one of the racers' engines started to smoke. It had blown!

A moment later, another race car blew an engine and skidded out of control.

Just then, a voice came through Mater's headset. "Get out of the pit—now."

Mater recognized that voice. "Hey, I know you! You're that girl from the party last night. You want to do our date right *now*?"

Mater left the arena to meet the pretty car.

Mater looked for Holley. She spoke to him over the headset when she saw him try to buy flowers. "No! Don't go in anywhere. Just keep moving."

Mater replied, forgetting that Lightning could hear him. "Stay outside. Got you."

Lightning was confused, but he moved to the outside of the track.

Meanwhile, Mater spotted Finn McMissile fighting the two tough cars from the bathroom.

Mater didn't know Finn was a secret agent. He thought he was watching a karate demonstration. He cheered them on.

Lightning told Mater to turn off the headset. Moving
outside had cost him the lead. He tried to catch up, but
another car won the race.

Afterward, Lightning was furious with Mater. "I lost the race because of you!"

Mater offered to try and fix things, but Lightning was too mad to listen. "I don't need your help! I don't *want* your help!"

Mater didn't want Lightning to lose any more races. He decided it would be better if he left.

The next morning, he went to the airport to fly home.

Finn McMissile went over to him, disguised as a security guard. "Come with me please, sir."

Finn knew that Grem and Acer, the two bad cars from the bathroom, were following Mater. They knew he had important information, and they wanted to get it back.

When Grem and Acer began to chase them, Finn told Mater what to do. "Drive forward. Whatever you do, don't stop." Finn fought off the bad cars as he and Mater sped out to a jet.

Holley was on the jet, too. They looked at a picture that the agent in the bathroom had given to Mater. Mater knew all about the engine they were looking at. Finn and Holley told Mater they needed his help for a top secret mission.

Mater agreed. "But you know I'm *just* a tow truck, right?"
Holley and Finn didn't believe him. They still thought Mater
was a secret agent—and a very good one!

The agents decided Mater should go undercover. "So I just go in, pretend to be this truck . . ."

Finn finished for him. "And leave the rest to us."

Disguised as a Russian tow truck, Mater snuck into a meeting of bad cars in Italy. He learned about a sinister plot to hurt the racers in the World Grand Prix. The bad cars were using radiation guns disguised as cameras to cause the racers' engines to explode. Mater realized that Lightning was in danger!

At that moment, Lightning McQueen was in Italy for the second race of the World Grand Prix. As the racers sped through the winding streets, another car exploded. The bad cars had struck again!

Mater knew he had to warn Lightning. But as he tried to leave the meeting, he blew his cover.

One of the cars spotted him. "It's the American spy!"

"Dad gum!" Mater made a quick getaway using some gadgets Holley had given him. Suddenly a parachute opened, and he flew off. "*Whoa-oh!* Wait!"

Mater hurried to the racetrack to warn Lightning. He pushed his way through the crowd, trying to get his friend's attention. "Let me through! You gotta let me in."

Before Mater could reach his friend, the bad cars captured him.

The next thing Mater knew, he was trapped. Finn and Holley were with him. They'd been captured, too.

Mater was upset. "This is all my fault. I'm not a spy. I really am just a tow truck."

This time Finn and Holley realized he was telling the truth.

The agents knew they were inside Big Bentley, a famous clock in London. Nearby, the final race of the World Grand Prix was taking place. Finn listened carefully. "Do you hear that? Those are race car engines revving in place. The third race hasn't started yet."

Mater realized he still had time to warn Lightning. He used the spy gadgets the agents had given him to saw through his chains. Then he raced off to save his friend.

After Mater had left, Holley used
her electro-shockers to turn
back the hands on the clock. She and
Finn escaped from the trap
and hurried after Mater. They
had discovered something terrible.
The bad cars had planted a bomb
under the tow truck's hood!

When Lightning saw Mater drive onto the racetrack, he forgot all about the race. "Mater! I've been so worried about you!"

Just then, Finn radioed Mater to tell him about the bomb. Mater knew he had to get away from Lightning. He began to drive backward. "Stay away from me!"

In the meantime, Finn and Holley began to capture the bad guys. But when more showed up, Mater's friends from Radiator Springs stepped in to help. Ramone spray-painted one while Guido pulled the tires off another.

But it was Mater who really saved the day. He figured out exactly who could deactivate the bomb. Everyone was safe!

The Queen of England was so pleased, she made Mater a knight. "I hereby dub thee Sir Tow Mater."

"'Sir'? You can just call me Mater, Your Majesty."

Soon Mater, Lightning, and the gang were back home. Best
of all, it had been decided that the last race of the World Grand
Prix would now be held in Radiator Springs. The race would
decide once and for all who was the fastest car in the world.

Lightning was happy, too. "No press, no trophy, just racing—the way I like it."

Just before the race, Finn and Holley showed up. Finn asked Mater to join them on a new mission. "Spy or not, you're still the smartest, most honest chap we've ever met."

But Mater didn't want to leave his friends. "Thanks. But as much fun as it was hangin' with y'all . . . this, this is where I belong." Still, there was one last thing he wanted to do. . . .

"Whoo-hoo!" Mater sped down the racetrack
until he was next to his best friend, Lightning.
"Check it out. They let me keep the rockets!"
"I'll see you at the finish line, buddy."
Mater grinned. "Not if I see you first."

Disney · PIXAR

Cars

AIR MATER

Read-Along
STORYBOOK AND CD

This is the story of Mater's adventure as a flying car.
You can read along with me in your book. You will know it is time to
turn the page when you hear this sound. . . . Let's begin now.

Read-Along Executive Producer: Randy Thornton; Read-Along Storybook Produced by Ted Kryczko and Jeff Sheridan; Adapted by Annie Auerbach
Illustrated by the Disney Storybook Artists. ℗ 2012 Walt Disney Records/Pixar © Disney/Pixar. All rights reserved.

One afternoon in Radiator Springs, Mater the tow truck was giving his friend Guido flying lessons. "Good, that's good. Now, give it more throttle."

Just then, Lightning McQueen drove up. When he heard what Mater was doing, he asked Mater how he had learned to fly.

Mater smiled. "You see it all started when I was towing this here car to Propwash Junction. . . ."

Propwash Junction was a town full of airplanes. Mater pulled into the town's service station to drop off the car he was towing.

Overhead, four jets thundered through the air. The jets left trails of smoke as they flew upward at an amazing speed.

Mater realized the jets were a famous team of stunt airplanes. "Wow! The Falcon Hawks!"

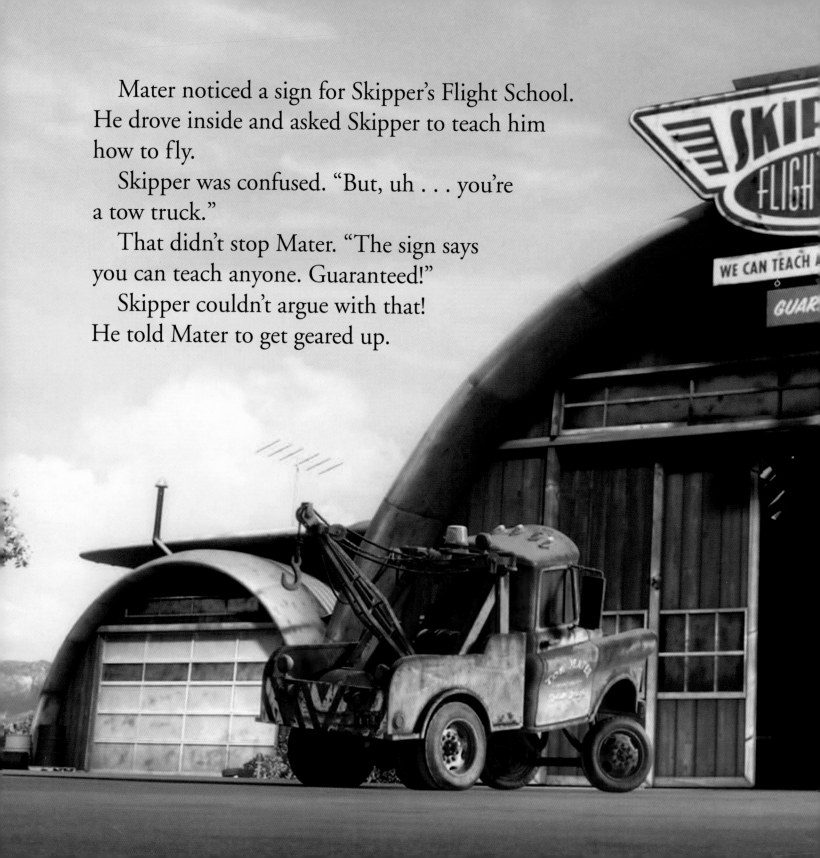

Mater noticed a sign for Skipper's Flight School. He drove inside and asked Skipper to teach him how to fly.

Skipper was confused. "But, uh . . . you're a tow truck."

That didn't stop Mater. "The sign says you can teach anyone. Guaranteed!"

Skipper couldn't argue with that! He told Mater to get geared up.

Before long, Mater was transformed into a rickety airplane. He had wings, a propeller, rudders, and a pilot's helmet. He couldn't wait to get in the air. "All right, let's do this!"

After a wobbly start, Mater was airborne! "Yeee-hooo!"

Just as he was getting the hang of flying, Mater caught
his tow hook on some telephone wires. He sprang backward
like a slingshot. "Wuh-uh-uh . . . Whoa!!!!"

But instead of crashing, Mater starting flying backward!
He was so proud of his new trick. "Look at me!"

Skipper was impressed, too. "I really can teach anyone!"

Meanwhile, the Falcon Hawks landed on a nearby runway. One of them had sprained his wing during practice, and the big air show was tomorrow! They had to find another stunt plane quickly—but where?

Just then, Mater flew right above the Hawks. They had never seen a plane fly backward before!

But Mater realized there was one trick Skipper hadn't taught him. "How do you land this plane?"

Mater *did* manage to land—upside down!

The Falcon Hawks were so impressed they asked Mater to join their team.

The next day, the air-show arena was packed with cheering fans. When the announcer introduced the Falcon Hawks, the crowd went wild and looked to the sky.

The stunt planes soared toward the stadium. Joining them was Mater. He had new wings, a helmet, and a slick paint job.

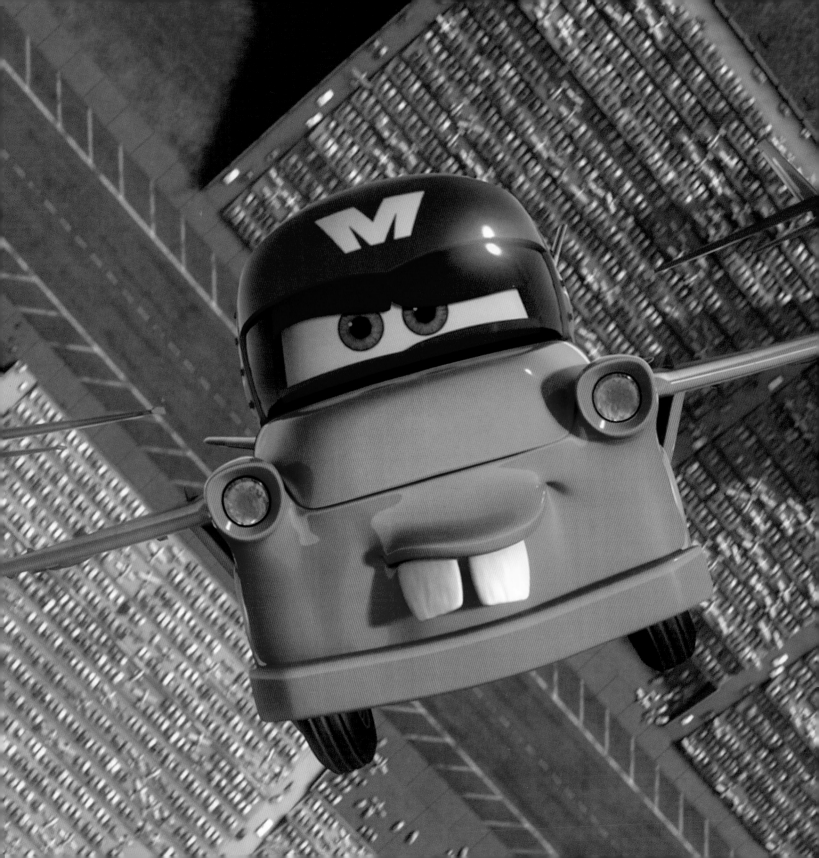

Mater and the Hawks swooped high above the crowd.
The fans in the stands loved it—especially Mia and
Tia. "Mater is awesome!"
Near them, Skipper watched, feeling very proud.

The Hawks split into
two groups, crisscrossing
paths on their way back up.
They created a tic-tac-toe
game out of smoke.

The announcer couldn't hold back his excitement.
"Tic-tac-*tow* Mater! That Mater Hawk is amazing!"

Next, Mater created a picture
of himself with his exhaust smoke.
The crowd oohed and aahed.
"It's a masterpiece!"

Mater

Now it was time for the grand finale. Red Hawk and Green Hawk flew toward Mater. They had a large elastic band in between them.

Mater gave the okay. "Mater Hawk is go!"

As he flew past the Hawks, he pulled the elastic band tight with his tow hook. Soon the band snapped back into place, and Mater hurtled backward through the sky.

Mater flew so fast that a giant BOOM
rumbled through the stadium. Skipper knew what
that noise meant. "He broke the sound barrier!"
"He's breaking the record!"

Unfortunately, Mater also started to tear apart! First, a metal bolt loosened and popped off. Then his helmet and wings sprang off. He spiraled down toward the ground. Mater tried to hold himself together. "I'm breaking up!"

Back in Radiator Springs, Lightning was worried. "Whoa! What did you do?"

Mater grinned. "Oh, you remember . . . Lightning McQueen Hawk!"

Outfitted with special wings, Lightning flew up to Mater. He caught the tow truck's hook, saving Mater before he crashed.

As Lightning pulled Mater through the air, he yelled to his friend. "All right now, Mater. Finish your finale."

Lightning let go of Mater's tow hook. "Okay, buddy, stick that landing."

As Mater dropped the short distance to the ground, he smiled at the stadium full of cheering fans. Then he touched down on the airfield and spun to a smooth stop at the end of the runway.

But Mater had one more
surprise ready for the last stunt.
He pressed a special button
with his tire, and fireworks lit
up the sky.

The crowd cheered! "What
a finale!"

In Radiator Springs, Lightning didn't believe Mater's story. "That did not happen."

Just then a call came in through Mater's radio. It was Blue Hawk. "Mater, we're down one plane. We need you, pronto!"

Lightning watched in shock as Mater and the Falcon Hawks flew away to another amazing stunt show!

Read-Along
STORYBOOK AND CD

Dusty Crophopper is an airplane with a very big problem—he's afraid of heights! To find out what happens when Dusty enters a high-flying race, you can read along with me in your book. You will know it's time to turn the page when you hear this sound. . . .

Let's begin now.

Read-Along Executive Producer: Randy Thornton; Read-Along Storybook Produced by Ted Kryczko and Jeff Sheridan; Adapted by Ellie O'Ryan Illustrated by the Disney Storybook Artists.

Dusty Crophopper spent his days flying over the crops of Propwash Junction, spraying them with Vita-minamulch. But in his dreams, Dusty soared higher, racing jets across the sky.

Leadbottom, Dusty's boss, didn't understand why Dusty wanted to race. "Pay attention! You're daydreaming again!"

Dusty tried to explain. "Look, I am more than just a crop duster. . . ."

Dusty wanted to compete in the Wings Around The Globe Rally, and the qualifying race was coming up soon!

Dusty's best friend, Chug the fuel truck, helped Dusty practice. "Okay, now let's try some tree-line moguls."

Even with Chug's directions, Dusty needed to go faster if he wanted to get into the rally. So Chug suggested a coach with some flying experience. "My buddy Sparky says the Skipper was a legendary flight instructor in the navy."

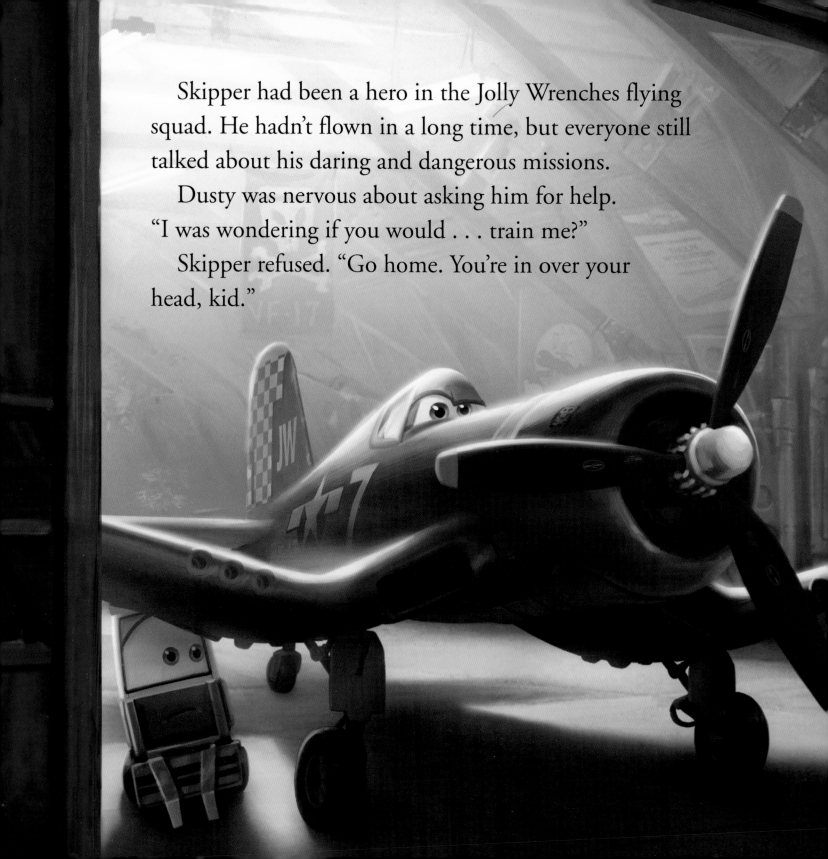

Skipper had been a hero in the Jolly Wrenches flying squad. He hadn't flown in a long time, but everyone still talked about his daring and dangerous missions.

Dusty was nervous about asking him for help. "I was wondering if you would . . . train me?"

Skipper refused. "Go home. You're in over your head, kid."

Dusty and Chug kept practicing anyway. Soon it was
time for the racing trials. Dusty flew as fast as he could,
but he missed making it into the Wings Around The Globe
Rally by a fraction of a second. Dusty sadly went home.

That night, a race official visited
Propwash Junction. He said that another
racer had been disqualified for cheating.
Chug cheered for his friend. "He's in!
Dusty's in the race!"

After hearing the news, Skipper decided to help Dusty get ready for the big race. He told Dusty all about cloud streets that would help Dusty reach top speed.

But when Dusty tried to fly higher, he got very scared. He told Skipper a secret. "I'm afraid of heights!"

"Scared of heights, and you want to race around the
world?" Skipper was shocked, but he decided he could
work around Dusty's problem. He taught Dusty to race
the shadows of high-flying planes so that Dusty could
stay close to the ground. They trained together every day
until it was time for the rally.

All of Dusty's favorite racing heroes were at the rally,
including Bulldog, Ripslinger, and Ishani!

Some of the racers, like Bulldog, weren't very friendly.
"This is a competition. Every plane for himself."

But one plane, El Chupacabra, was excited to meet
Dusty. "We will have many adventures, you and I! I will
see you in the skies, amigo!"

Soon the first leg of the race began. The planes zoomed off toward Iceland.

But Dusty didn't try to climb as high as the other planes. As he glided just above the Atlantic Ocean, he flew into a fierce storm. Then, he had to swerve around huge icebergs!

Dusty wasn't the only plane having trouble, though. During the next leg of the race, Bulldog sent out a call for help. "Mayday! Mayday! Mayday!"

Dusty zoomed over. "Apply your left aileron. Stop roll. Now quick, pull up!"

Dusty guided Bulldog to a safe landing. "Thanks for your help, matey." Bulldog didn't understand why Dusty had slowed down to help him, but he was still grateful.

The next part of the race was to India. Dusty surprised everyone by moving up to eighth place. His fast flying and kind actions earned him fans all over the world!

But Ripslinger was not one of those fans. "Why are they wasting their time with him? He's a tractor with wings!" Ripslinger thought that crop dusters shouldn't compete with real racing planes.

With just two legs left in the race, Dusty moved into second place! But the next flight, across the Pacific Ocean, would be long and dangerous.

Before the race, Dusty radioed his friends in Propwash Junction. Skipper was especially worried. "Be careful."

Before they hung up, Chug had some big news to tell
Dusty. "We're going to meet you in Mexico!"
Dusty was so excited! "Really?"

However, before Dusty could reach Mexico, one of Ripslinger's teammates broke Dusty's navigation antenna! Dusty flew for miles in the wrong direction. He was about to run out of gas when two navy jets approached.

Dusty asked them for help. "I'm running on vapors. I-I need to land!"

The jets led Dusty to the *Dwight D. Flysenhower*—Skipper's old ship! On board, Dusty saw the Jolly Wrenches Wall of Fame. But only one mission was listed under Skipper's name. Dusty was sure it was a mistake.

The navy planes refueled Dusty before he took off again. But soon, Dusty was caught in a terrible storm! He was too scared to fly above it, so he was badly damaged. He barely made it to Mexico.

When he landed, Dusty talked to Skipper. "One mission?"

Skipper finally told Dusty the truth. On his first mission, his team had been in a terrible battle. Skipper lost many of his friends. "After that, I just couldn't bring myself to fly again. I'm sorry, Dusty."

Dusty felt like giving up. He had so many broken
parts that he didn't think he could finish the rally.

As Dusty thought about dropping out, Ishani rolled
by to wish him luck on the race. But she wasn't alone!

A huge group of racers arrived, pulling carts loaded with new parts for Dusty. El Chu even brought a pair of new wings! "Amigo, I cannot bear the thought of competing without you."

Dusty was so grateful.

Soon, Dusty was running better than ever. He was ready to hit the skies for the last leg of the race. But Ripslinger still wanted Dusty to lose.

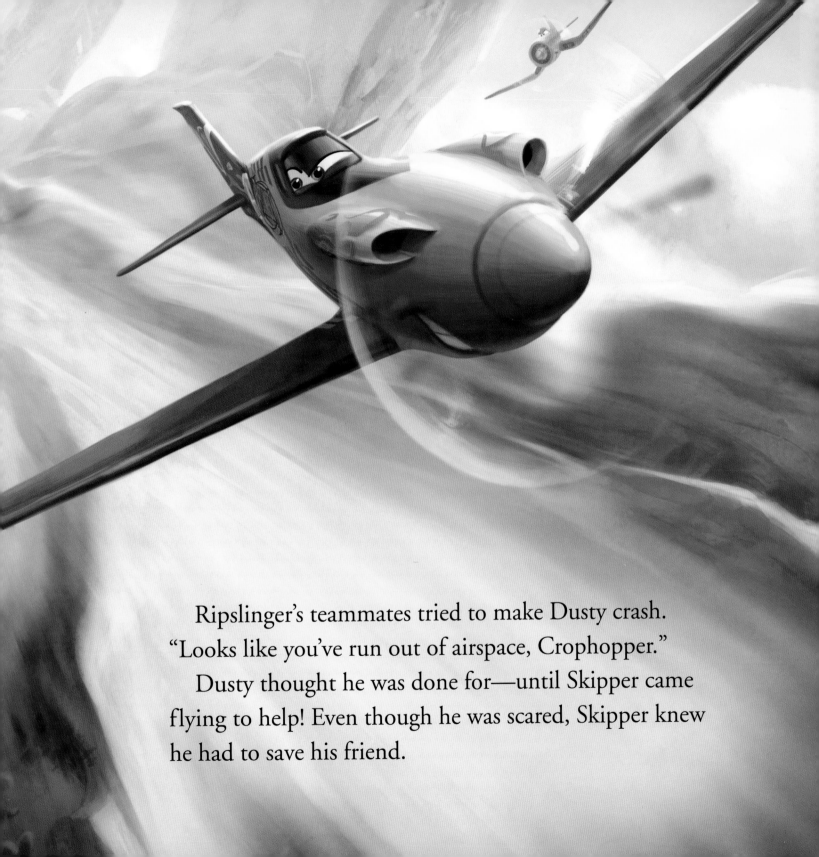

Ripslinger's teammates tried to make Dusty crash.
"Looks like you've run out of airspace, Crophopper."

Dusty thought he was done for—until Skipper came flying to help! Even though he was scared, Skipper knew he had to save his friend.

Dusty caught up to Ripslinger, but he couldn't
go fast enough to pass the champion plane.
Dusty looked up and saw a fast cloud street
overhead. "Don't look down. Don't look down!"
Taking a deep breath, he flew higher and higher.
"Oh, yeah! *Whooo-hoooo!*"

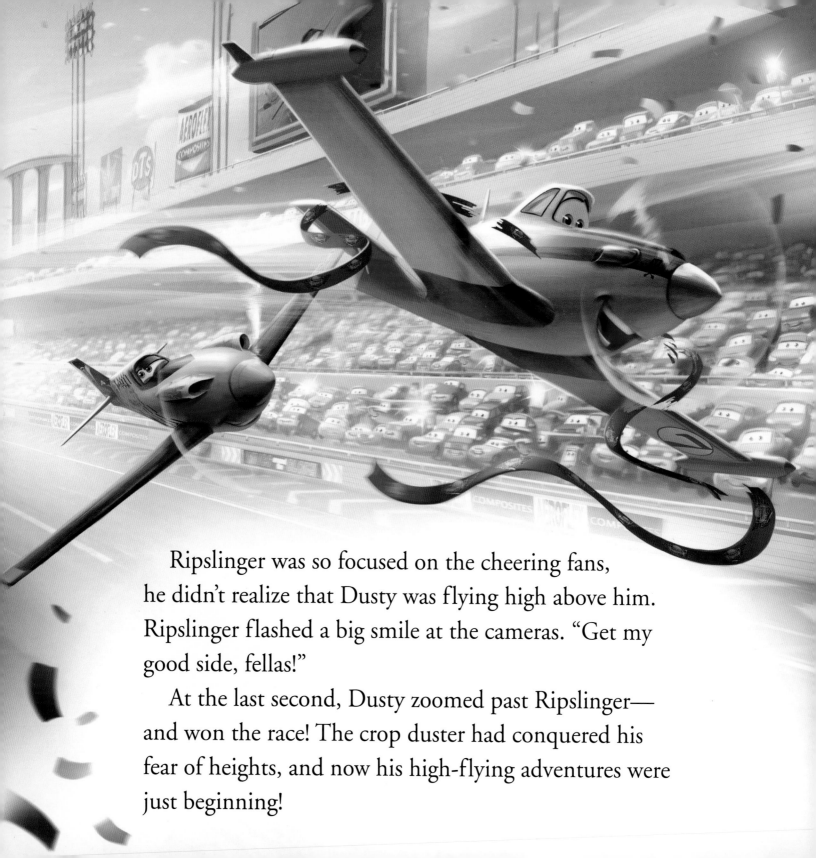

Ripslinger was so focused on the cheering fans, he didn't realize that Dusty was flying high above him. Ripslinger flashed a big smile at the cameras. "Get my good side, fellas!"

At the last second, Dusty zoomed past Ripslinger— and won the race! The crop duster had conquered his fear of heights, and now his high-flying adventures were just beginning!

Narrator: **David Jeremiah**
Featuring the voice talents of:
Not Chuck: **Mike "No Name" Nelson**
Lightning McQueen: **Owen Wilson**
Mack: **John Ratzenberger**
Sheriff: **Michael Wallis**
Mater: **Larry the Cable Guy**
Doc Hudson: **Paul Newman**
Sally: **Bonnie Hunt**
Luigi: **Tony Shalhoub**
Flo: **Jenifer Lewis**
Additional Voices: **Kathy Coates**
Kori Turbowitz: **Sarah Clark**
Bob Cutlass: **Bob Costas**
The King: **Richard Petty**

Narrator: **David Jeremiah**
Featuring the voice talents of:
Lightning McQueen: **Owen Wilson**
Mater: **Larry the Cable Guy**
Acer: **Peter Jacobson**
Gren: **Joe Mantegna**
Holly Shiftwell: **Emily Mortimer**
Finn McMissile: **Michael Caine**

Narrator: **David Jeremiah**
Featuring the voice talents of:
Lightning McQueen: **Keith Ferguson**
Mater: **Larry the Cable Guy**
Skipper: **Stacy Keach**
Mia: **Lindsey Collins**
Tia: **Elissa Knight**
Judge Davis: **Jonathan Adams**
Blue Hawk: **Lori Alan**

Narrator: **David Jeremiah**
Featuring the voice talents of:
Dusty Crophopper: **Dane Cook**
Leadbottom: **Cedric the Entertainer**
Chug: **Brad Garrett**
Skipper: **Stacy Keach**
Bulldog: **John Cleese**
El Chupacabra: **Carlos Alazraqui**
Ripslinger: **Roger Craig Smith**

For information, address Disney Press, 1101 Flower Street, Glendale, California 91201.

ISBN 978-1-4847-0656-5
F383-2370-2-14066

Printed in China

First Edition

1 3 5 7 9 10 8 6 4 2

For more Disney Press fun, visit www.disneybooks.com.